When Teddy
Woke Early

QUALITY TIME BOOKS™

TEDDY TALES:
Teddy in the Undersea Kingdom
Teddy's Christmas Gift
When Teddy Woke Early
Teddy and the Chinese Dragon

Library of Congress Cataloging-in-Publication Data

Mogensen, Jan.
  When Teddy woke early.

  (Teddy tales) (Quality time books)
  Translation of: Har du sovet godt, Bamse?
  Summary: When he falls from the bedroom window while Max his owner is
still asleep, Teddy finds a way to get back home with the help of friends he
meets along the way.
  [1. Teddy bears — Fiction. 2. Friendship — Fiction. 3. Self-reliance —
Fiction] I. Title. II. Series.
  PZ7.M7274Wh   1985   [E]   85-26096
  ISBN 1-55532-007-4
  ISBN 1-55532-006-6 (lib. bdg.)

North American edition first published in 1985 by

Gareth Stevens, Inc.
7221 West Green Tree Road
Milwaukee, Wisconsin 53223, USA

First published as *Har du sovet godt, Bamse?* by Borgen with an
original text copyright by Jan Mogensen.

Typeset by Ries Graphics

English Text: MaryLee Knowlton

When Teddy Woke Early

Jan Mogensen

Gareth Stevens Publishing
Milwaukee

The sun wasn't up yet but Teddy couldn't sleep.

"I'll wake Max," he thought. "We can play!"

Teddy tickled Max's nose. But Maxie just twitched and turned over.

"Well, *I'm* getting up!" Teddy said.

Teddy climbed to the toyshelf.

"I'll need this hat, and the drum, and the sticks," he told
the puppet and the soldier. "Let's make a parade."

But it was just too early. The puppet and the soldier
weren't ready to play either. So Teddy made a parade of
one.

Back and forth he marched on the window sill, high
stepping and beating his drum.

Suddenly he stumbled and fell backwards out the window.

Down, down, down Teddy fell through the morning silence.

Whoomp! Crash! Teddy landed on a large sleepy black cat.

The cat awoke in a fright. She hissed. "What are you doing here, Teddy?"

"Well, I know what I *was* doing," said Teddy, "but I'm not so sure what I'm doing now. I think I would like to go back to bed."

"Well, since I'm up, I can take you part of the way," said the cat. "Hang on tight!"

With Teddy on her back, the cat leaped to the top of a
wooden fence. She walked carefully to the end. Teddy
hung on tight. He was too scared to look up.

At the end of the fence the cat jumped.

"This is as high as I go," she said. "I'm going back to
sleep."

And she left Teddy at the top of the house next door.

The big black cat was gone.

Teddy sat down on the roof looking up at his open window.

"Max will be up soon," Teddy told himself. "He'll miss me and come looking."

But time passed slowly and Teddy grew lonely. And tears began to run down his face.

Just then, a voice came from behind Teddy. "What's the matter, little bear?"

Teddy turned and saw two squirrels watching him.

"I want to go home!" he cried. "But I can't reach my window."

"Oh!" said the squirrels. "We can help you get to the top of the lamp post."

The two squirrels helped Teddy climb up through the tree.

The wind made strange whistling noise through the leaves. Teddy's fur stood on end. "Are there ghosts in this tree?" he asked.

But the squirrels were busy chattering about something else and they didn't answer.

At last Teddy and the squirrels reached the top of the lamp post.

"Good luck!" called the squirrels. And they disappeared back into the tree.

Teddy looked around him, trying hard not to cry again.

He saw that a wire stretched from his lamp post over to the window of Max's room.

"This I must do by myself, I guess," he thought.

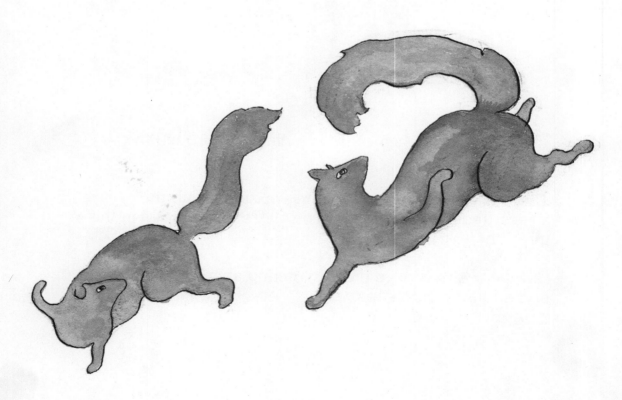

Carefully Teddy lowered himself to the wire.

Slowly, one step at a time, he began to cross over to the window.

Taking short steps, first one foot, then the other, he was almost home. Then suddenly, one foot slipped! Once again, Teddy was falling.

At that terrible moment, a pigeon flew by. Swooping swiftly, she grabbed Teddy by the seat of his pants.

In a flash, she flew back up to Max's window and dropped Teddy on the sill.

24

"Thank you for saving me!" Teddy said, hugging the pigeon.

"My pleasure," said the gentle bird.

Teddy waved good-bye as the pigeon flew off into the morning sun.

Teddy had just crawled back into bed when Max awoke.

Max looked out the window at the morning sky.

"It's a beautiful day, Teddy," he said. "Are you ready for some adventures?"

Teddy didn't budge. "Not likely!" he thought.